LEARNING
SEVENTEEN

LEARNING SEVENTEEN

Brooke Carter

orca soundings

ORCA BOOK PUBLISHERS

Library and Archives Canada Cataloguing in Publication

Carter, Brooke, 1977-, author
Learning seventeen / Brooke Carter.
(Orca soundings)

Issued in print and electronic formats.
ISBN 978-1-4598-1553-7 (softcover).—ISBN 978-1-4598-1554-4 (PDF).—
ISBN 978-1-4598-1555-1 (EPUB)

I. Title. II. Series: Orca soundings
PS8605.A77777L43 2018   jc813'.6   C2017-904481-8
C2017-904482-6

First published in the United States, 2018
Library of Congress Control Number: 2017949720

Summary: In this high-interest novel for teen readers, Jane finds
her soulmate at a Baptist reform school.

MIX
Paper from
responsible sources
FSC® C016245
www.fsc.org

*Orca Book Publishers is dedicated to preserving the environment and has
printed this book on Forest Stewardship Council® certified paper.*

Orca Book Publishers gratefully acknowledges the support for its
publishing programs provided by the following agencies: the Government
of Canada through the Canada Book Fund and the Canada Council
for the Arts, and the Province of British Columbia through
the BC Arts Council and the Book Publishing Tax Credit.

Edited by Tanya Trafford
Cover image by iStock.com and Shutterstock.com

ORCA BOOK PUBLISHERS
www.orcabook.com

Printed and bound in Canada.

21 20 19 18 • 4 3 2 1

For Tia, who stayed with me in the rain.

Prologue

Hannah always said, *Everyone has a story to tell. You're the star of your own life's journey.* I thought that was both adorable and cheesy as hell. It turns out she was right and wrong—I *do* have a story to tell, but the truth is, my life didn't really even start until she showed up. The day she walked into the gray walls of New Hope Academy with her wild red hair and her loud voice and curvy body was the day I started living. This might be my story, but she was the star.

I'm getting ahead of myself. If I'm going to tell this story, I'll have to go back to the time before Hannah. It's hard to think of those days. I was so lost and just waiting for someone to find me. Looking back, I hardly recognize myself. But there's something good to be found in all this, I know it. If I can change, and if Hannah could have loved the messed-up person I was, then who knows? I might have a future after all. You might too. Whoever you are, I hope this story finds you the way Hannah found me. I hope it lifts you up. I hope you'll see the truth in it. I hope you'll see that things can get better. Even for people like you and me.

Chapter One

Intake at New Hope Academy—or, as I like to call it, No Hope—is a lot more boring than it sounds. The word *intake* seems like it might be about getting something, but really it's about taking things away. They take you away from your home, from your friends, from your old school, from your neighborhood, from sex (especially the "unholy"

3

kind), from junk food, from television, from the sweet smell of marijuana, from staying out all night, from doing whatever you want whenever you want, from your favorite low-cut top, from your angry music, from your weird dyed hair, and from everything that makes you, well, you. After all, Baptist reform schools put a pretty heavy emphasis on the "reform" side of things.

When you walk into these unremarkable yet somehow threatening walls, they take your temperature, your medical history, your allergies, your past, your present, your future, your bad attitude, your lack of faith, and they write it all down. Oh, they love to write things down. I think they do that so they can hold your sins against you.

They want to tear you down so they can build you up fresh. I know their game. I see how it works on the others, all the sad little boys and girls who get sent here because their mommies and daddies just can't deal anymore. I see how it works on the meek little girl they pair me up with as a roommate-slash-cellmate. Marcie, her name is. Might as well be Mouse for the squeak of her voice. So timid she can't even look me in the eye.

The people here think I'm just like Mouse on the inside, a good girl waiting to get out, but their Find-Jesus program won't work on me. No, I'm a different species altogether. If Mouse is a rodent, then I'm the cat. I wonder how long it will take them to figure it out.

My stepmonster, Sheila, convinced Dad that No Hope is their last hope at straightening me out, so to speak, so they're dumping me in here along with all the other unwanted weirdo kids. Dad didn't even take time off from work to attend my "intake" and left it up to Sheila to get me settled. I guess her idea

5

of "settled" means pushing me inside the front doors and then speeding off in her Acura.

I've been through the "orientation" process, which is really just a rundown of the rules (spoiler alert—there's a lot of them). I have a couple pairs of scratchy skirted uniforms and a blank journal, and I am now sitting here in my cell.

The room has linoleum floors and two single beds, one for me and one for Mouse, and the walls are decorated with paintings of Jesus that look like they were done by some teenager who was locked up here in the '70s or something because ol' Jesus is throwing down some sweet rock-and-roll hair. For some reason, none of the paintings show a whole-body shot. Each image is of a different part of his body. Dismembered Jesus really gives me the creeps.

Over my bed is a painting of his hands, palms up, the skin color a little too yellow and the nail-wound blood a little too pink and applied too thick on the canvas, as if the artist thought piling on the paint would make their total lack of talent less obvious.

There is a painting of his eyes, all sad-like, over Mouse's bed.

The top of sad Jesus' head with his overgrown mullet hovers over the doorway. That one has a crown of thorns and a halo. I think either one would have been enough, but what do I know?

And then there's the one of his feet. Oh, the feet.

They look just like I always imagined God's feet would look like. Huge, wide, stubby-toed white feet in strappy brown-leather sandals with flat soles. When I first saw the painting I had to sit down on the squeaky little bed because just looking at it made me feel dizzy.

It's true, I thought. God really is a foot.

You see, when I was a little kid I asked my mom (my REAL mom, not the stepmonster) about God and she told me that he was everywhere and that he could see everything. I said he must be really big to be everywhere at once, and Mom agreed.

I remember we were standing in our backyard and the wind was blowing the sheets on the clothesline. I said that I bet God's big toe was about all that could fit in our yard with us. Mom didn't say anything, and I looked out over the lawn and the trees and the fence and where the blue of the sky met the horizon and I felt like you do when you're about to cry or fall asleep. I swear I could see God's giant foot, transparent but there, really there, just hovering over my house and my street and my neighborhood.

Momma, I asked, *why doesn't he step on us?*

She just laughed and laughed.

Chapter Two

The No Hope Journal of Jane Learning
Entry #1: Lies, Lies, Lies

I am supposed to write in this stupid
journal if I ever want to get out of No
Hope. That's RULE NUMBER ONE of about
a zillion different NOs and DO NOTs. Today
my counselor, a really squirmy-looking
guy named Terry, asked me to think about

the nature of lies. He wants to know what I've learned about my behavior since I got here. I don't really think I've learned anything, except how to bend the rules (and that if you're a real pain in the ass, your family will just ship you off to live with Jesus freaks).

But I guess I do know something about lies. If you lie to someone, then they can't love you and you can't love them because you're not being your real self. You may think you love each other, but it's all an illusion. It took me a while to understand this. What surprises me more is that the adults at No Hope haven't figured out the truth-love connection yet. They're all walking around like they've got the truth in their pockets. But if you ask me, they're just spreading more lies.

Here's an example. Let's say you are hanging out with someone you really like a lot and they invite you to meet their family and you suddenly realize that you are girlfriend material. Like, you are being considered for an honest-to-goodness role in this person's future and so you start imagining that future. You can see it all—how this girl you like will become someone you really love, and then your ultrareligious stepmonster will know that you are definitely, absolutely not straight. Then she'll force you to break up with the only girl who ever loved you and your life will be over, and you'll learn the hard way that people who live in truth tend to die alone. Lies are so much more attractive. Yes, lies are safer.

Back to that hypothetical meeting with your new girlfriend's parents. What if this cute girl's liberal-yet-suspicious dad asks you an innocent, run-of-the-mill question like, "Have you always lived in the area?" Instead of saying yes and admitting your local status (because maybe he'll run into your parents), you find yourself saying something crazy about how actually you were born in Budapest, and as soon as the word is out of your mouth you regret it. You really have no idea why you said it, except that, oh yeah, you are a totally compulsive liar.

So now you are committed, and there's no greater commitment than a liar to her lie. And you rack your brain at their raised eyebrows and you search your memory for plausible details the way any good liar would do, and all you can think of is Hungary. Budapest is in Hungary.

Then a lightbulb pops off in your brain and you see the fourth-grade class photo illuminated in your internal gallery of pictures. And third from the left—spotlight on, zoom the camera in—is your fourth-grade bestie, Anna Pusky. Oh, good old Hungarian Anna, with her dark hair and dark eyes and European skin tone. So you try to embody Anna and conjure her within yourself. You imagine the smell of pig-snout stew and imagine your stepmother as Mrs. Pusky, with her weird fur hats, her accent, and her penchant for oversized amber-colored glasses. You imagine, as any skilled liar would, that feeling these details will somehow transmit them through you as a kind of truth, like method acting, and you can see by the lowering eyebrows of your dining companions that it is working. It's *working*.

You hope now that no one asks too many probing questions because, frankly, you don't know a damn thing about Hungary. And there it is. Now that you've lied, you can never love this girl and she can never love you. You probably won't be able to see her again after this because if you got more serious then she might ask a question and you'd have to admit to the lie.

With each passing day, week, month, the chances of being found out escalate. It has already gone too far, let's face it—it has already gone *way* too far to admit the truth now. Because it's too weird to be a joke, right? Saying you were born in Budapest when you weren't is just too weird to be a joke, and no one would ever understand why you'd lie about such a thing.

Now whenever you hear the word *Budapest* or think the word *Budapest*, you will be reminded of the lie. You will be reminded of saying goodbye to that girl, that potential great love. *Budapest* will now equal goodbye. Then years later when you're old and alone you will go to the doctor and they will only have bad news. That lie you told grew inside until it invaded your cells, and now it is stuck deep inside, way back in the hardest-to-reach area, way back past your heart, and it's pushing for your death. It wants it. It can't be cut out. You can't be saved. The lie can't be taken back. *Budapest, Budapest, Budapest*, it throbs

in your blood. *Budapest*, you dumb girl.
Budapest, you liar.

Is that what I am supposed to say?
Did I get it right? Can I go home now?

Chapter Three

You're probably wondering what I did to get sent here, right? Well, it wasn't just one thing, and it also was just one thing. I know—nothing is ever simple with me. I've been messing up for a long time in lots of spectacular ways, but I guess the one major way I've been messing up is by having a thing for other girls. I mean, it's not just a

passing phase. It's not just a prefer-
ence. I've tried being with guys, and
that's sort of okay, but when I dream
about love, I dream about loving a girl.

Dad and Sheila have put up with
a lot of my shenanigans, but if there's
one thing my stepmonster can't live
with, it's having a lesbo stepdaughter.
I think she tried to ignore it for a while,
but when I got caught making out with
Jenny Flaherty, shirts off and all, in the
equipment locker at my old high school,
well, she just couldn't take the embar-
rassment. So they sent me here to No
Hope. Yay me.

After a few weeks I find I'm
getting used to this place, and I hate
that. I am getting used to the smell of
lemon-scented floor wax, the sounds
of rubber soles on linoleum and sobs
into pillows, the taste of warm, recycled
air rebreathed by all the other messed-up
kids. The kids who stare out windows

that don't ever open. I'm used to it the way I am used to not getting high. I have no choice, and so I live with it. But I'm the kind of person who doesn't get used to things easily.

Keeping my journal and doing the lame writing exercises they ask me to do is supposed to be therapeutic, but really, it's just making me mad. I mean, I don't think my counselors want an honest answer. All they want is for me to tell them how wrong I am. I think asking someone to list their faults and all the dumb things they've done in their life is just cruel. After all, have you never done anything wrong? Have you never made a mistake? You know what? If you haven't, then I don't want to know you. But I do know that if I want to get out of here, I have to play along.

So I pretend to reflect back and figure out what went wrong. I bet they're looking for some trite confession, some equation of wrongdoings and low self-esteem that will add up to a picture they can understand. But they'll never understand. How can they? And anyway, maybe I'm just a bad girl. Maybe I am evil. That's what they want me to say. I'm evil because I like girls.

Today I meet again with counselor Terry, and I shudder as I walk into his office. It smells like feet and beans. Terry is a tall skinny guy with a pointy, pinched face and a long nose. I think he looks like a really gangly bird, and his tuft of almost-white blond hair adds to the effect. Baptist Big Bird. He smiles when I walk in, but it's one of those smiles that doesn't touch the eyes, so I know he's faking it. I mean, how could he possibly be happy to see me? I've only been here a few weeks and already I'm a huge spear in his side. Ha.

He sighs when I sit down, and I sigh back, mocking him.

"How are you, Jane?" he asks, shuffling the papers around on his desk. "Any journal entries for me?"

I hand over my journal, and he leafs through, taking a few minutes to read. After a while he stops. "You know," he says, "this won't work if you don't take it seriously."

I shrug. "How can I? I don't believe any of this Jesus stuff."

He bristles at that. "Maybe a little faith would do you some good."

"Meaning?"

"Meaning if you put your trust in the Lord, you might find freedom from your sins. Jane, it isn't your fault that you're...you're different."

"You mean gay?"

Terry coughs. "You're not gay, just confused."

I roll my eyes. "No, Terry, I'm not confused."

"That's Satan at work in your life," he says. "You need to ask God for forgiveness."

"So I just ask to be forgiven and that's that?" I ask.

"Well…yes," says Terry. "And then you must try to never sin with other girls again."

I laugh. "Oh, Terry," I say. "Keep dreaming, man."

We go back and forth like this every time we see each other. I really wonder why he doesn't give up. He goes on and on about "good" selves and "bad" selves. I really think he believes I have a demon in me or something. I mention this to him, and he says he thinks I exaggerate to amuse myself. I tell him there's nothing funny about any of this but that if I don't laugh, I'll probably die in this place.

Every time I see him, he asks me if I want to be saved. I always tell him the same thing. But I don't think he believes me. I tell him it's all I've ever wanted.

Entry #2: What Came First

I am supposed to start with my family. What family? We're broken, not together anymore, not really. Eggs. I think it all started with eggs. I remember Mom rushing down the stairs. I was carrying a plate with a half-eaten bacon and egg sandwich on it. I was ten, I think, and Mom and Dad had been having their nasty arguments ever since the baby died. Even though it wasn't really a baby yet.

Anyway, I could hear them banging the cupboard doors and smashing the plates, and I figured I should go up to the kitchen and put my plate away because then they'd probably stop for a little while. Mom would be sitting on the kitchen counter in her dirty old jogging suit, crying while she drank her coffee from the special mug with her name on it. *Elsinora.*

We had to have that mug specially made because we could never find one with her name on the rack at the drugstore. Maybe that's why she gave me such a regular name. Plain old regular Jane.

Just below the rim of that mug there'd always be a stain of hot-pink lipstick. A permanent record of Mom's kiss, like a fingerprint. I used to say that if she ever went missing all we'd have to do was give the cops that mug.

So yeah, she scared the crap out of me flying down the stairs and I dropped my plate and I expected her to yell, but instead she grabbed me and squashed me into her chest really hard.

I noticed that she wasn't wearing her regular clothes. She was wearing jeans and pumps and a leather jacket, and she pushed my head so hard into her shoulder that I felt my nose crack a little.

The pain shot through my cheeks and all I could smell was blood and leather and her cheap drugstore body spray. The skin of her neck was all warm and soft. She whispered in my ear.

All I could think about were the little skin tags on her neck and how she always told me that I would twist on them as a baby and try to pull them off.

She whispered goodbye to me and then pushed me away.

That's when I noticed the duffel bag on the step behind her. She grabbed it and went out the door.

My fat old mutt, Chrissy, waddled to the top of the steps and woofed at me. I asked her what the hell she was looking at and then threw the plate at her.

It's funny. I always thought it would be my dad who left.

Eventually, after months of radio silence, Mom sent me a collectible spoon from San Francisco. I tried to imagine my mom in San Francisco but her face kept getting more and more out of focus until she was just this faceless body hanging off the back of a streetcar, and I kept imagining the body falling off and getting run over, so I had to stop thinking. Sometimes I have to take the pictures in my brain and tear them up and make them disintegrate into nothing because I just can't take thinking about things anymore.

Like eggs. I can't eat them anymore since I learned about the life cycle of chickens. At school we put some eggs into an incubator to see if they'd hatch into cute little chicks. We learned about what the eggs were made of and how baby chickens form, and I remember I started feeling sick and couldn't believe I had ever eaten an egg before.

There is this thing called a snow embryo that you can sometimes see when you crack an egg. It's a little white globule near the yolk that would turn into a chicken if it was allowed to be fertilized and live.

I remember thinking about Mom and the baby she was supposed to have. I wondered if it was bigger or smaller than a snow embryo. I wondered if Mom ever thought about getting me cut out while I was still a globule. Dad always said that kind of thing is a sin. I guess that's why he was so mad at Mom for it. Maybe that's why she left, I don't know.

Entry #3: Enter the Stepmonster

My counselor wants to know about Sheila. Here's what I know about her— not much. Sheila is the ultimate closed book. When Dad first got a girl-friend after Mom left, I was pretty excited. Then I actually met Sheila the Baptist. I remember asking her what a Baptist was, and she said it was someone who was BORN AGAIN in Christ. She told me that if I wanted eternal life, all I had to do was ask Jesus to forgive me and he'd come into my life and make me whole again.

I said, "That sounds pretty good, but how do you do it?"

She said, "Pray."

One night, not long after they were married, Dad and Sheila went on a date to a movie. When they left, I sat in the rocking chair and prayed out loud.

"Hi, Jesus," I said. "Want to come into my life?"

I kept thinking I'd feel something, like a warm glow or a spark or a shock or something. But I didn't feel anything. Nothing at all. I knew then that Sheila would never love me. How could she? God didn't even want me.

Chapter Four

Perhaps you're wondering if everything about No Hope is awful. Yes, yes, it is. Well, I guess my roommate Mouse is okay. She's basically mute, so at least it's quiet. My classes are boring because they spend less time on traditional subjects and more time on Bible study. We're most definitely not being taught about evolution in science class, and my English class has really boring books with no sex or murder in them or anything that could be considered anti-Christian in any way. Honestly, I don't mind some of this God stuff, but do they have to be so hard-core about it?

When we have lunch in the cafeteria, we have to have a group prayer beforehand. When we play volleyball in gym class, we have to have a group prayer beforehand. It just never ends. And none of these people ever seem to get tired.

So today I have a free hour of time to go to the library and generally do what I want. I guess a few weeks at the school without making too many waves means they are letting their guard down around me. That's good. I can use that to my advantage.

The school itself is pretty big. One block on the north side holds the dorms for the residential kids (the naughty ones like me), and one block in the south houses the classrooms. They are connected by a long corridor where the main administration and counseling offices are. The gym is to the east, adjacent to the cafeteria and library.

You want to know something really shocking? Some kids come here *voluntarily* and are happy to bus in and out every day. Seriously, there is a large courtyard at the front, next to the most important building on campus— the chapel—and every morning and evening the buses roll in and out so that all the kids can attend services. We also attend services on family visit days.

Sheila is always getting mad at me when we are at the school church on family day because I won't sing loud like this other girl, a popular chick named Nicky Huffton. She is in my youth group and sings in the youth choir and she always has rosy cheeks and bouncy hair and trimmed nails.

She sings cheesy, New Age-y, pop-style Jesus songs at the pulpit with a microphone while her mom gestures and sings along from the front pew. I'm sure you can guess—she is one of the kids who wants to come to No Hope on a bus.

The Hufftons are like my parents' idols. Mrs. Huffton runs all the women's ministry stuff, and Mr. Huffton is the head deacon. Nicky sits straight up in her pew like there is a rod up her butt and the whole family makes a big show of getting all moved and weepy during the sermons—especially when Pastor Jim is at the pulpit.

Pastor Jim is the head Jesus-thumper. He's this mysterious guy we never really see until the congregation needs baptisms or fresh bouts of brainwashing. Pastor Jim looks like a real Baptist should—skinny (not gluttonous) and bearded (wise), with straight white teeth (for all the smiling), and dressed entirely in beige clothing (like Jesus). The thing about Pastor Jim is, when he gets going on a sermon he can really rile the congregation up. When he leads us all in prayer I like to keep my eyes open a tiny bit so I can look around at everyone's faces. They are all fakers. Some look rapt, some look like they are going to cry, some smile and nod, some look peaceful, some even look angry or like they are going to give God a great big fist bump any second. Some, like Sheila, make little *hmm* noises and whisper *yes* and *Amen*. They're the worst.

One time at youth group, we all had to take turns leading the group in prayer, and when it was my turn I blew them all away when I asked the Lord to MAKE US MORE LIKE JESUS. Oh, counselor Terry was tickled by that one, I could tell. If there's one thing I'm good at, it's imitating. My real mom always said I should be an actress.

Nicky Huffton totally hates that I am so good at memorizing scripture. Ever since Sheila gave me my own Bible, I've been devastating the youth group with my readings. It's yellow, that Bible, and it has a picture of a young Jesus surrounded by children and baby animals. Sheila asked me to memorize the entire Psalm 23. You know, the one that goes "The Lord is my Shepherd, I shall not want." My favorite part is the whole "walking through the valley of the shadow of death" thing. I love anything dark and dramatic.

I can rip through that psalm, adding inflection and drama at the good parts. I say it for Sheila and then she leaves me alone for a little while. You do what you have to, you know?

Entry #4: The Girl Who Corrupted Me

Terry keeps asking me who my first lesbian crush was, and it's starting to get weird. I mean, is he getting off on this? I told him it was Wonder Woman, but he wants to know who the first girl I ever "sinned" with was. Well, here you go, Terry.

It was Lisa Cork. She lives across the street and is a year older than me. She thinks that makes her way more mature and she treats me like I don't know anything. I don't mind because mostly she is nice and she always has cigarettes. She steals them from her stepmom and we go smoke and talk about how we hate our stepmoms. Sometimes we make out. I'm not really that attracted to her because she is super petite, and I like bigger, stronger-looking girls. I don't even think Lisa is exclusively into girls, but I don't exactly have anyone else to make out with.

I'm pretty sure I am her type though. I've never had trouble attracting girls or guys. I'm pretty tall, and I've got some curves, and I was blessed with the same dark mane of glorious hair my mom has. Top that with my big green eyes and I have everything I need to get my way.

Chapter Five

"So, Jane, I've been reading through your latest journal entries, and I have to say..." counselor Terry starts and then trails off.

"Say what?" I ask.

"Uh, well..." He shifts uncomfortably in his seat. His office is decorated in various Bible-themed crafts, no doubt given to him by the countless delinquent kids he's saved from hellfire.

"You have a unique point of view. Do you ever feel like you are alone?"

"How do you mean?" I ask. "Of course I am alone. My family kicked me out and put me in Jesus prison."

"Reform school," corrects Terry. "And we like to think of this as a place of love, a place where you can blossom into the young woman you're meant to be. A young woman who follows in the footsteps of Christ."

I make a gagging noise, and I see that Terry's face is flushing red. I'm getting a rise out of him. Good.

"Jane, don't you want to be happy? What would make you happy?"

"I will be happy when I walk out of this place and never come back."

Terry nods. "I'm sorry that you just don't seem to be engaging with the program."

"Well, Terry," I say, "I hate your program, so…"

"Jane, you will never be free without Jesus."

"Are we done here?"

"Fine," says Terry, tossing aside my file. "Just do me a favor, okay?"

"What?" I ask.

"Can you just not scare the other kids? You're making some of them uncomfortable."

"How do you mean?"

"We've just—we've gotten some complaints that you are whispering threats during study time, and one girl thought you were staring at her in the bathroom."

"Right," I say, anger rising in my chest. "Because I am a huge, evil lesbo? It's so goddamned typical. I didn't do anything!"

"Language! Now, that's not—"

"Whatever, Terry. I get it. Everyone hates me, I'm a lost cause, I'm going to burn forever." I get up and go to the door. "I've been keeping to myself this whole time and you people still won't let me be."

"Jane, wait," he says. "Just try, okay?"

"Terry, man, all I ever do is try," I say. "I've been trying my whole life. I'm done with that."

"You understand we will keep you here for as long as your parents want. This isn't going to be a quick stay."

"What?" I whirl around.

"You're not eighteen yet, so you'll be here as long as you're a minor."

"But…I don't turn eighteen for like six more months."

Terry shrugs, and I swear I see a little smile play across his face.

"Go to hell, Terry," I hiss.

I walk out the door and make sure to slam it hard behind me.

I'm so mad that by the time I have to attend mandatory Bible study, I've decided I am going to seduce Samantha (who everyone calls Sam), the semi-hot senior with the shaggy, sandy hair and a swimmer's lean body. She has soft brown eyes and even softer-looking lips. Since they already think I'm making passes at every girl in the school, I might as well live up to their clichéd expectations.

I can tell Sam's into me even with the ugly, boxy uniform they make us wear. I play with the way it hangs on my body and roll up the waistband on the big pleated skirt so it's not so long. I always stand with one hip out to the side so she can see I have a shape. I let the buttons of my shirt gape a bit so she can see my skin all white and creamy against the rough fabric.

The other kids here are prudes. Half of them are here because they want to be, and that means they've barely even kissed yet. Take Mouse. I bet she doesn't even know what kissing with tongue is like. The other half of them, the supposed bad kids, aren't even that bad. One girl is here because she got too many Cs on her report card. Another one had a party while her parents were away, and some stuff got broken. So far I don't talk to anyone except Mouse, and that's only because of proximity. But I know that stories about me are getting around. Good.

Here I am in the middle of it all, a shark in a guppy tank. That's something Sheila used to say to me after picking me up from the principal's office when I'd done some bad thing or another.

She hasn't come to visit since the first few Sundays. You know how some people are lapsed Christians who only show up on holidays or when they need a favor from God? Well, Sheila is a lapsed parent. Dad calls once a week, but that's it. I think Sheila wants him to forget about me. Occasionally Dad sends me letters that Lisa Cork has given him. She puts puffy stickers on them and scratch-and-sniffs, which I like. I sniff until I feel like I'll get a nosebleed. The best one she sent was a giant pickle sticker.

At night I take the pickle out of its envelope and press it to my face, inhaling its synthetic tartness. It smells so much like the real thing that my mouth starts to water. I think about what's real and what's not. I wonder how much of life is a real pickle and how much is just a sticker that smells like one.

Chapter Six

In the mornings we have group therapy and play all these dumb trust games. Like the one where you fall backward and have the other person catch you. The first time didn't go so well.

Nicky Huffton and I went first. In some misguided statement about the social politics of this place, Terry thinks that if he can just pair up the perfect

Christian female specimen (her) with the hellbound (me), somehow Nicky's chastity will transfer through to me. Or we'll become friends like they do in bad '80s movies, and all will be well, and I'll start wanting to wear pastels and bake stuff. The problem is, it will never happen.

Nicky looked over her shoulder at me and whispered, "Don't drop me, bitch." So what could I do? I had to live up to her expectations. I took a little step to the side and she sailed on by. I watched her eyes get bigger at the moment she realized I wasn't going to catch her. It was all I could do not to step on her face once she was on the floor.

It was funny until I realized I was the one who had to fall next.

Today, after the trust games, we toss eggs. Some break and get on the floor, but we wipe them up with paper towel. I get paired with Sam, and we manage to toss the same egg to each other twenty-three times before it breaks in her hands. I can see that she's happy to be playing with me.

Then Pastor Jim tells us a story about this couple who have a whole bunch of kids and are expecting another one, but they don't have any money, and the doctors tell them the baby is probably going to be blind, deaf and mentally disabled.

Pastor Jim asks, "What would you do if you were them? Would you have an abortion?"

"Yes," I say.

"No!" The word flies from every other mouth, and all eyes turn to me. Even Sam looks at me with disdain.

Pastor Jim points his finger at me. He says, "You would have just killed Beethoven."

They all seem like they are a hundred miles away, the black-and-white linoleum hypnotizing me, making my eyes blur. It is in this moment that I know I have to get out of here. I don't belong. I will never belong. I have to find a way out.

It's late. I meet Sam behind the chapel stage. I think she's excited about sneaking from her dorm.

We don't talk. I take her by the hand and lead her through the corridor to the baptism pool. It's like this awesome, deep hot tub that they always have going because kids get baptized every Tuesday night.

I don't know why it's Tuesdays and not Sundays, but during these services some kid who has found Jesus witnesses to us all and gives their life testimony. It usually isn't all that interesting. Maybe they cry, or maybe they smile the whole time. But they always look so sure, with

Jesus brand-new in them. They believe it all so through and through that they're going to ask to be washed in the tears of Christ so their soul can be protected for eternity.

It's sick how all these kids are afraid of dying now, afraid of a hell they didn't think about before coming here. The kids who have been saved, well, they watch while this other one gets dunked by Pastor Jim and comes up all sputtering and clean. The other kids raise their arms up over their heads like they're at a rock concert, but I want to yell at them to stop being so stupid. They're all a bunch of fakers anyway.

I don't want to witness or testify or ask for my soul to be saved and I sure as hell don't want skinny Pastor Jim to be touching me with his skeleton hands in the hot tub while I'm all wet and he's all wet. But I have no problem doing that with Sam.

"Come on," I say, leading her down into the water.

She gets all goofy and shy and scared, like she's not sure we should be doing this, but I take off my top and she changes her mind. She walks in after me, still wearing her whole uniform.

"Ugh, it's lukewarm," she says, and I laugh. But the word strikes me. *Lukewarm.* Pastor Jim told us how God welcomes the hot and the cold but spits the lukewarm out of his mouth.

"Are you hot or cold?" I ask.

"What do you mean?"

"For God. Hot or cold?"

"Neither, I guess. Stop being weird."

She wades over and puts her arms around me. While she's kissing me, all I can think about is that Bible passage Pastor Jim mentioned.

"I'm the cold," I say.

Here I am in this baptismal tank, in a chapel where other kids commit their on-fire souls to God, with a girl who doesn't know what she's doing, letting her go as far as she wants. All I can think about is how cold I am.

Chapter Seven

After the night in the baptismal tank, I decide I'm not that into Sam anymore. She isn't a great kisser and she's too shy to go all the way.

Bonus—I discovered how easy it is to sneak out. No one is really watching the kids that late at night. Most of them are too scared to leave their rooms, but I'm not.

As soon as lights go out, I make Mouse promise not to tattle and then sneak down the corridor to the outer doors. I hike up my skirt and make a run for it, climbing the chain-link fence at the back of the property and slipping into the trees.

The night is cool and damp. Early fall. When I'm outside, I feel so much more like me. Other humans need all the comfort and convenience of malls and houses and beds and stuff like that. I just want to be alone with myself in the wild. Maybe I'm meant for another time, another place. Maybe it's here that's the problem and not me. Maybe it's the when of it all that makes me stand out so much.

I feel powerful as sticks crunch under my feet, as I step over logs and feel my muscles loosen from being so wound up. I think a lot of girls would be scared to be alone at night in the bushes, but not me. I'm never scared.

Once I feel like I'm far enough away, I cut a line toward the highway to catch a ride.

It's not long before two guys in a Mustang stop to pick me up. I get in, and one of them hands me a beer.

"I dig the uniform," the less-good-looking one says.

I smile at them and can see the driver eyeing me in the rearview mirror. I sit back and relax into my seat.

"Where's the party?" I ask, and the guys laugh.

"Our place," says the driver. "You'll see."

They're right. The house is at the end of a long farm road and is crawling with people. There are cars all over the property and groups of girls and guys drinking and fighting and partying in every room.

The driver tells me his name, Rob, and leads me by the hand to the kitchen. He gets me another beer.

A guy offers us some white powder and I snort it right off his hand. I don't even care what it is. Rob doesn't want any, and then I'm thinking maybe I shouldn't have snorted it because he's pretty hot and he's older and kind of nice so far and I don't want him to think I'm a stupid kid. It's bad enough that I'm wearing the uniform. Then I get even more nervous when I find out his band is playing at the party, and he's the guitar player.

But soon I don't care, because the drugs start to kick in. Rob's playing with his band and it sounds good and he keeps smiling at me and there's just something about him with his clear, open blue eyes and nice smile and I just almost can't take it. I have to get some air.

I go out back. People are hanging out on the porch, and some are chilling around a bonfire. I walk over and stare at it. I see faces in the fire looking back at me.

Time stops.

I can see every atom and molecule at once and then nothing at all. I panic for a second, thinking I'm going blind, but then my sight comes back to me, more brilliant than ever. I can see tiny bugs crawling through the grass toward the fire, like some mass insect suicide.

As I'm watching, I see something a few inches larger moving toward me from the fire. I walk closer and see that it's a salamander. I pick it up, expecting it to disappear, but it's there and it's in my hand and it's pretty big and I don't know where it came from. It couldn't have been in the fire.

Then someone says, "Hey, does that girl have a lizard, or am I just tripping?"

And then a bunch of people are looking at it and touching it and all of a sudden I start to panic a little.

I'm afraid all of them touching it is going to hurt it or kill it somehow, like how touching a butterfly can kill it because it loses its special flying dust or whatever. Then I'm laughing because that's a funny idea, and I start thinking about angels and how they can fly and if they're covered in dust and you see one then you shouldn't touch it in case you kill it. Then I stop laughing because I start thinking about the nature of the universe and how nothing is what it seems and maybe angels don't have wings and don't look like people and instead come in the form of salamanders. This salamander could be an angel, and all these people are trying to touch it and kill it.

I back away, shaking my head. "No, you can't touch angels or they die."

"What did she say? That chick is screwed up, man. She's all talking about angels."

"It's mine!" I yell, and I run with the salamander to the road.

I need to find a safe place for it, but everywhere I look there is a group of people who could hurt it. I just can't let it go into the ditch because that's an awful place for an angel to have to live and I haven't figured out what it means and what if it's lonely or scared or what if it comes looking for me and gets run over, and soon I'm crying.

I'm just sitting in the road and I'm crying and I can't stop. I can't breathe. The salamander is just sitting in my hand, looking at me, my tears falling onto its iridescent skin.

I cry because the salamander has no place to go. I cry because it's in love with the world and wants to experience it, but the world doesn't love it back. The world just wants to touch it, to molest it until it can't feel anymore.

"Hey there. Hey now. Hey you." A soft voice is beside me. It's Rob. "Want to come inside? You can bring your lizard."

"It's an angel."

"You can bring your angel too."

I turn to thank him, and then everything goes black.

Chapter Eight

I stay with Rob and his friends for a couple of days. They're actually really nice. They drink a lot, but none of them make a move on me, and Rob doesn't expect anything. He drops me off in town at the mall and tells me to call him if I need help.

The mall in town is pretty small, and there are not many people there at 10:30 AM. My clothes are kind of ratty because I haven't been at school for...how long has it been? I wish my hair wasn't so greasy and that I didn't have so many bruises from wandering in the bush and falling down at the party. I should be way more upset about it, but it's helping me look pitiful.

At first I just walk into the food court looking like I am lost, but I know exactly where I am. I really want a hot dog. I mean, a hot dog and a coke is about all I need in the universe right now. A hot dog and a coke will solve all my problems. A hot dog and a coke, and I can die satisfied.

So I sit down near the yellow counter of the hot-dog joint and watch its rolling seduction of wieners. I just sit there salivating over it.

When I know the cashier is watching, I dig into my pockets and pull out my ninety-seven cents in change and count it out all slow. When I tally it up and then look at the menu board for the price, I almost squeeze out a tear. I walk up to the counter and pretend to be a shy girl down on her luck. Only part of that isn't true. That is the key to a good lie. Remember Budapest? You have to have something true to cling to.

When the cashier—Betty, according to her name tag—walks over to me, I give her a little smile, and I can see from her face and the downturn of her chin that it is working, and she is feeling sorry for me. I look from the drink cups to the wieners to my fistful of change and back again.

"How much are the wieners?" I ask quietly.

She says, "A couple of bucks."

I look in my fist and say, "Oh. Can I have a small coke then?"

She says sure and gets it for me, and when I count out my change she looks over her shoulder and says, "You know what? It's on the house. Would you like a hot dog too, honey?"

I say, "No thanks, I couldn't."

She says, "Oh, you look like you need it."

I say, "Thank you so much. You are so nice." I get my hot dog with extra mustard and my coke, and I don't pay a cent. I wish I could say I feel bad about it, but I'm just so hungry. Add it to the list of my sins, No Hope Academy. It must be getting pretty long by now.

After a few days of bumming around, I head home to Dad and Sheila's place (I've already stopped thinking of it as being my house too). But I'm there just long enough to clean up and grab some things. I know if Sheila comes home and sees me there will be screaming. And if Dad comes home and sees me there will be disappointment. I can't handle either of those things right now.

I go into the bathroom and turn off the light, because I don't want to see myself in the mirror with my dirty face and dirty hands and dirty teeth and dirty insides. I turn on the shower full blast and take off my clothes.

I open the shower curtain and step inside, but I don't get under the spray right away. I stop just shy of the water and watch it go down the drain all clean and fresh. I guess I don't want to mess it up because I just stand there shivering outside the warmth in the strange wind that rises up from the rush of falling water. The warm meets the cold and I get all goose-pimply and I want so bad to step under the spray, but I don't let myself.

I feel the dirtiness on me, in me, and I know it won't matter how clean I get on the outside. I'm always going to be dirty to people like Sheila and the No Hopers.

I finally step under the stream, and it is so hot I want to jump away. But I don't. I let it scald my scalp, my face, my arms, my chest, my legs, my feet. I take the loofa from the shelf and scrub. It hurts, but I don't care.

I dress in fresh clothes, layering them so I can go a while without having to come back. Then I go to the kitchen for supplies. I put some Spaghettios and a can opener and a knife in my backpack.

I hear a sound behind me as I'm digging through the cupboards, and there is Sheila. She's looking at me like I am some alien creature. Then Dad walks in.

Suddenly it is just a chorus of voices, everyone getting louder and louder except me, because I never have anything to say.

"Jane!" Sheila shrieks. "What do you have to say for yourself?"

They always ask me what I have to say for myself, but there is never an answer, and they don't understand that. What do they want me to say? That I'm bad and inconsiderate?

I look at Dad, and he just looks so disgusted with me.

"I know how rotten I am inside," I mumble.

"What?" he asks, his face registering concern.

Sheila jumps in before I can answer him. "You think life is this big party. Well, I've got news for you! You're nothing special, and the sooner you realize that, the better."

"Sheila—" Dad starts, but she cuts him off.

"No, John! You don't know what she puts me through with her late nights and the drugs and God knows what else. She has no respect."

"What do you want me to do, Sheila? She's my daughter."

Great, now I've caused another fight. It seems like everywhere I go, I cause trouble for people. My dad isn't a bad guy, and he deserves to be happy. The problem is me.

"I don't want you to keep doing this," I say softly, and they both turn to look at me.

"What does that mean?" Sheila snaps.

"Fighting over me," I say.

"Jane—" Dad starts.

Sheila cuts him off again. "Oh, don't worry, Jane. We won't. As far as I'm concerned, we're done with you. You're not welcome here."

"Sheila!" Dad shouts, but I'm already out the door and don't hear what comes next. I don't want to. It's clear that I need to go. I have no one and nothing. There's really only one thing left to do.

I run out the front door, and my stomach hurts so bad from eating so little that I feel like I am going to puke. Then I get very dizzy and actually do end up heaving. I only manage to spew a bit of yellow sludge on the front step.

I'm scared because I am sure, certain beyond all doubt now, that God does not exist. So if he's not the one punishing me, then I'm doing it to myself. I wish my dad would just forget me. His life would be so much easier. I wonder if I will be able to forget myself.

Chapter Nine

This girl Maggie I met at a party has a place near the highway where she says I can crash, so I walk there with all my stuff in a garbage bag. It takes a couple of hours because it's so late at night and there aren't any cars wanting to pick me up.

Maggie is only seventeen too, but she has her own place because she got some money from a car accident that made her lose a big part of her calf muscle. She says it hurts a lot, and I bet it does. Part of me envies her having her own apartment, but I don't think I'd want a scar that big on my leg. I don't say this to her because I don't want her to kick me out.

There are a couple other people staying here too, and the only place left to sleep is this big closet near the front door that is pretty deep and carpeted all the way in. Maggie loans me a pillow, and I use my hoodie and jean jacket as a blanket. When I shut the folding doors from the inside, the light disappears one sliver at a time. It is pretty neat lying in here while everyone comes and goes. I just watch their feet and try to sleep.

One night this guy they call Newfie comes over to Maggie's with some good acid, which he gives me for free after

I promise to kiss him. I do, and it isn't so bad, even though he does have ashtray breath.

After everyone is asleep or passed out, I sit on the small third-floor balcony and look out over the parking lot that spans the housing complex and the bar next door. I swiped some bubble-blowing solution from the dollar store earlier, along with some Tootsie Rolls that I kept for my dinner. It's freezing out, but I don't care. I dip the wand into the pink bottle and blow.

Pop. Try again. *Pop.* Go slower. The bubbles look amazing as they grow. They start as film and then grow when I push air at them, and then they come together in these perfect spheres and suddenly I am remembering math lessons that I kind of miss because I'm not in school. I start to feel bad so I blow another bubble.

I blow so many bubbles that the entire neighborhood is blanketed in them.

I don't know if it's the cold or that it's nearly dawn or if I'm just tripping out, but the bubbles stay put. They aren't going away. They cover cars and cement and awnings and balconies and bikes and yard toys.

Pretty soon I run out of bubble solution, so I get some dish detergent and shampoo and use that, and the bubbles come out bigger, thinner, grayer, meaner, harder, like bubbles on a coke binge or bubbles that have to sleep in closets or bubbles without real moms. The sun is rising and all the colors wash over the bubbles and they change from silver to blue to red to orange to green and back again.

As I blow them, each one carries away an image of my face, mouth pursed, hair wild, a bruise on my cheek, like I am caught in some perpetual mirror screaming, "No!"

All the bubbles float down from the sky onto the sleeping world, each one filled with my breath, a piece of me. I watch as the world stirs and the first people shuffle groggily from their front doors to get into their cars to go to work. They are expecting to see the same old gray world they always see and to meet the same gray day that never changes.

But today is a day covered in bubbles, and so their faces are soft and they all smile, and some look up to where I sit on the balcony, and some see me and some recognize that the day of bubbles is my day. My gift to the world.

The next day I steal several boxes of Gravol from the drugstore. I see them on the shelf and I just start shoving the boxes into my hoodie. I tell myself that I didn't plan this, that I'm not going to do anything stupid, but I steal them anyway. Some part of me knows what

I am going to do. Even the dog sitting across the street staring at me knows. I'm not sure if it is a real dog, because I shoved all the pills into my mouth a few hours ago before I could change my mind and it might be a bad thing because I keep seeing dogs everywhere and they all have these bright blue eyes that follow me.

They're not mean dogs, but they don't blink, and I don't know if I have ever seen so many in one day before. It's like all of nature is watching me. When I walk down the street the bushes pull away like they are recoiling from a flame, and I swear I can hear them breathing out oxygen. I wish I had a friend with me for this. The bushes and the docks and the rocks and the raindrops and the clouds and the sun and the trees and the grass all know the truth about me and what I am doing.

In the dark place there is no light. I am not afraid of the space around me. It is not like deep water. It is not cold. From the infinite a voice speaks to me, but it has no sound. It only talks to me in feelings, and for the first time ever those feelings don't hurt. It says everything will be all right. It says, *I forgive you*. It says, *I love you*. I wonder if it is God, but then I realize that is impossible. I want to stay in the deep darkness. But someone keeps shaking me.

In the room the wallpaper is a forest. Trees tower over me and cover the ceiling with a green canopy. I try to imagine the smell of bark and stump and rot and rain, but all I smell is antiseptic. I see cartoon animals on the walls. I'm in a bed. I am holding my breath and then coughing. A long tube comes from my throat.

Then a woman with short blond hair is standing over me. She wants to talk to me. It really is not a good time to talk. She says that if she were in my place, she would cry.

"But I'm not you," I say. So I don't cry.

What comes next are fragments. Shoes squeaking, white pills, yellow pills, charts, frowns. A cardboard meal, a plastic fork, paper pyjamas, daytime television.

Being an expert-level screw-up has fringe benefits, apparently. I kind of tried to kill myself but failed at that too. Now they'll all think it was a cry for help. That's the worst part. I don't really want to die. I just want them to leave me be.

What's my prize for surviving an evil Gravol trip? My shattered dad in my crappy hospital room. The best worst thing I've ever won. When he comes in he looks like a shadow, so gaunt and scared and dark around the eyes. But he's here. He doesn't talk. He just holds my hand. Sheila comes, and she stands by my bed and watches me. She does not hold my hand.

Once the drugs are finally clear of my system and I am deemed "out of the woods," it looks like I'll be taking another long vacation at No Hope. I bet they've missed me. I sort of miss them in a sick way. That's the thing about not being a kid anymore. You still need a home, but no one thinks you're cute enough to give you one. There are no sweet puppies at this pound. Just ugly, kicked-around ones that bite.

Chapter Ten

When you almost kill yourself and then end up back at Baptist reform school, they have a tendency to go extra heavy on the reform. The overall rule is that until I'm deemed less of a "danger" I can't leave my room except for class or meals or to use the bathroom. To be honest, that is fine by me. I don't want to socialize. I just want to lie in bed and sleep.

The other thing that's different is that I've been assigned a new counselor, a psychologist named Dr. Lamp. Apparently, counselor Terry was just barely adequate and took a leave of absence. The new counselor is supposedly the bee's knees, as Nicky would say, and has a much higher success rate with curing kids of their various evils. He'll have his work cut out with me. I'm meeting with him later today. But until then I'm staying in bed.

Mouse has been scurrying around me, casting anxious glances my way as if I'm going to jump up and infect her with suicidal tendencies at any moment.

"Mouse," I croak, my throat still sore from having a tube stuck down it. "What did I miss while I was gone?"

"Her," Mouse squeaks.

"Her? Who?" I ask.

"You haven't seen her? She's across the hall. She's enormous."

"What? Mouse, are you saying a giant moved into No Hope while I was, um, indisposed?"

Mouse shakes her head. "Not a giant. A star. Like, someone who could be an actual celebrity one day."

I laugh. Mouse is a tabloid junkie, and her contraband is forbidden at No Hope. "Really? A celebrity?"

"You'll see," says Mouse. "She's cinematic."

"What are you, in love? Joining my team, Mousie?"

Mouse frowns. "No, I just wish I was like her," she says sadly.

"Come on, Mouse. God made you perfect, don't you know?"

She shrugs.

"Well," I say, "let's see this 'star' of yours."

Curiosity has always been my downfall. I drag myself out of bed and open our dorm-room door. The door across the hall is ajar, and so far I see nothing amiss. I listen and can hear the faint sound of someone whispering. But then a blur of red curly hair comes barreling out and nearly knocks me down.

"Whoa!" I yell, and then, because yelling hurts my throat so much, I start coughing. Then, because coughing hurts so much, I have to go sit back down on my bunk. I feel so weak.

"You. Are. A. Legend," says a honey-slick voice. I finally look up, and I swear my heart stops for a moment.

Standing over me is the most magnificent redheaded specimen I have ever seen. She is tall, broad-shouldered, curvy as hell and practically vibrating with kinetic energy. Mouse was right. Cinematic.

"Um," I start, not normally at a loss for words. "What?"

"You're Jane, right?" asks the red goddess.

"Y-yeah. And you are?"

"Oh. I'm Hannah." She plops down next to me on the bed, and her scent wafts over me. It is a refreshing mixture of green apple, vanilla, body heat and the sweetly seductive scent of girl. I take a deep breath, and my head spins.

"Whoa, you okay?" Hannah asks.

I nod and then lie back on my bunk. I don't want to pass out. My whole body is buzzing.

"I heard you had a little brush with death."

I look at her, angry for a minute, and out of the corner of my eye I can see Mouse shrinking back like she knows I'm going to blow. Who does this Hannah chick think she is anyway?

"Whoa, don't get mad," Hannah says, reading my mood. "I just...I've been there, you know?"

I look at her, into her impossibly huge brown eyes that are so dark and deep I can hardly see the pupils, and I can hardly see the pupils, and I can see that she is sorry. She does know. I decide to change the subject.

"What's this *legend* business?" I ask, trying to regain my composure and some semblance of an upper hand.

Hannah smiles. "Rumor has it you're the naughtiest girl at Hopeless," she says.

"Hopeless." I chuckle. "That's even better than No Hope."

Hannah shrugs. "I have a way with words."

I nod, impressed. "Mouse here," I say, "does not."

Hannah throws her head back and laughs. The sound fills the room.

"I know," she says. "I've been trying to engage Marcie in conversation ever since I transferred in a few weeks back. No dice."

"Transfer?" I ask. "That's a thing?"

"Oh yeah," says Hannah, leaning in closer. "I got sent here because they couldn't get me to play along at the last school. I'm afraid I'm a terminal case."

"Terminal?" I ask. "What's your sin of choice?"

Hannah chuckles. "No sin, Green Eyes." She gets up and walks to the door, and I can't help but watch her hips sway. She turns back to look at me and flashes me another smile. "I just love girls is all. I love them, they love me, and that is never going to change. I especially have a thing for girls with green eyes."

She walks out, leaving behind her fresh scent and several long red hairs on my bed. As she travels down the hall, I can hear her softly singing a folksy tune. "*Beautiful, beautiful green eyes…beautiful, beautiful gree-en eyes…I'll never love blue eyes again…*"

And just like that, Jane Learning is in love. Hopelessly, dangerously in love.

Chapter Eleven

I'm still riding on a Hannah high when it's time for me to meet with Dr. Lamp. I pump Mouse for information as I hurriedly change clothes and smooth my hair. That's one of the RULES here—you have to "maintain an appearance of tidiness at all times"—and even though the last thing I want to do is meet another Jesus-thumping counselor, I am too tired to put up much resistance.

Mouse has a surprising amount of intel on Hannah Henriks—that's her name, and I think I will start calling her Double-H, at least in my own mind. Or maybe Double-Hot...I don't know. It seems Mouse is quiet but cunning. She is an expert-level eavesdropper, and once I get her to open up her tiny mouth, a veritable flood of gossip comes out.

Apparently, Hannah has been to several reform schools, and her family tried No Hope in a last-ditch attempt to cure her of her horrible case of the "gays"—as if that would even be possible. She's hooked up with girls at every institution and openly breaks the rules and resists the Bible teachings.

"Wow," I say to Mouse. "Hannah's kind of my hero."

"There's more," says Mouse in her squeaky way.

"Do tell," I say as I grab my journal and walk to the door.

"There are rumors that she's totally insane." Mouse's eyes widen.

"Crazier than me?" I ask and crack a smile.

"You're not crazy, Jane," says Mouse. "You're just sad."

I look at her for a minute, like I'm seeing her for the first time. She's right, but I don't tell her that. I just nod and walk out the door.

This day is getting kind of intense, and I haven't even started my *PSYCHO-*therapy session yet. As I walk up to the counseling offices, I see that Terry's name placard has been scraped off and a new one rests on the floor beside the door, just waiting to be placed. It reads *Dr. Jacob Lamp, PhD*.

I walk up to the door and lightly rap.

The door swings open, and I come face-to-face with a tiny little man with white hair and a full white beard. He looks like a miniature Santa. For a strange second I am kind of scared that this is God in disguise.

The tiny man clears his throat and pulls a roll of breath mints from his pants pocket. He pops one in his mouth and offers one to me.

"Uh, I'm cool," I say. "I don't normally eat things that strangers offer me."

The tiny man cocks one eyebrow. "I'm Dr. Lamp, but you can call me Jake, so I'm not a stranger." He grins. "And anyway, I thought you had a real habit of taking things strangers give you. That's why you're back here, isn't it?"

I haven't even set foot in his office and already he's analyzing me and

calling me on my shit. It's both infuri-
ating and refreshing. This guy doesn't
mess around.

"You don't waste any time, huh?"
I say.

Jake smiles and steps aside,
motioning for me to enter.

"I'm not much for small talk," he
says. "Occupational hazard."

I walk in and sit down, then place
my journal on his desk.

"What are you doing?" he asks.

"Um, turning in my journal for
review."

Jake looks stunned for a minute.
"Why?" he asks finally.

"Don't you…don't you want to read
it? Terry always read it."

Jake shakes his head. "I would never
do that," he says. "That's your journal.
No one is going to read it unless you
want them to."

I reach over and take it back. "Okay," I say.

We sit looking at each other.

"You have a question?" Jake asks.

"If you don't read my journal, how will you know if I've been cured?"

Jake chuckles. "Well, I'm pretty sure I can predict the future on that point. You will not be cured. Not now, not ever."

I stare at him in stunned silence. Who *is* this guy?

"Jane, this is a Christian academy, so we do have certain beliefs here. And a lot of those beliefs conflict with what is best for my patients. To me—and, frankly, to the head pastors here— what is most important is that the youth staying with us feel loved and safe. We've made some changes around here since you've been gone."

I nod, taking this in. "But what about the parents?" I ask. "What about my dad and Sheila? They're paying a bunch of money to keep me from being gay."

"Is that right?" asks Jake. "Do you think that's what both your parents want? Your dad? Maybe he just wants you to be safe and doesn't know any other way. Is that possible?"

I think about it. "Yeah," I say. "I guess. But Sheila, she's more worried about how she'll look than about my future."

Jake nods. "Maybe. And maybe she just hasn't figured out how to be a mom yet. Why not give her a chance?"

I shrug. "Why can't she give *me* a chance? I still don't understand why she thinks being a lesbian is a choice. I mean, things have been really hard for me. Doesn't she think I would have chosen to be straight if I could have? If you had asked me a few years ago, I would have jumped at the chance to be 'normal' for a change."

"And now?" he asks.

"Now I'm not so sure. Being gay or queer or whatever you want to call it just kind of works for me. It fits, you know? I mean, it's lonely a lot of the time. But also, it just feels right. Especially when I meet someone…" I trail off.

"Someone?" Jake asks.

I blush. And then I spill. For some reason, I trust this guy. "There's a girl here," I say. "Hannah. She's…beautiful and…different. I don't know how to describe it. She just has this energy."

Jake nods. "I get it. She's a firecracker, that one. I felt like that when I met my wife," he says.

"Am I in trouble?" I ask.

Jake shakes his head. "How can loving someone be wrong, Jane? It's your behavior that matters. I know you think this God stuff is baloney. I don't care about that right now. I care about you.

I want you to keep your head straight so that when you get out of here in a couple of months, you'll be in a good position to lead a happy life. And, hopefully, you'll have a decent relationship with your parents. Sometimes playing along gets you farther than resisting."

I consider this. "Okay," I say. "I think I could try."

"What are your goals, Jane?" Jake asks.

I shrug. "I just want to be free, be happy. I want to be in love."

Jake smiles. "Those are good things." He takes a breath. "But you need to be careful with Hannah."

I look at him. "You don't want me to be with her."

"No, that's not it. Hannah is not well."

"What do you mean? She's sick?"

"I can't say much more," says Jake. "Just…be careful."

"Okay," I say.

"Good," says Jake. "Now, hurry out of here and go to class. You need to buckle down if you have a hope in hell of graduating."

I stare at him.

"Yeah, I know," he says. "I said hell—get used to it."

I walk out with my head spinning. This Jake guy is kind of nuts—in a good way. But what did he mean about Hannah? You know what? I don't care. Love can't be bad, right?

I feel a renewed energy as I walk down the hall to my English class. I hope Hannah is in my classroom right now, waiting for me. I hope I get to sit beside her. I'm going to get my work done and get decent grades and try to follow the stupid rules so that when I get out of here, I can do whatever the hell I want with whoever I want.

Chapter Twelve

It turns out that Hannah *is* in my English class. And my science class. And gym class, and study period, and youth group. She isn't in group therapy with the rest of us, which I think is weird. She has her own private counseling sessions with Jake, and afterward she's usually happy and light, like she's filled with extra air. Sometimes she seems really down, and I find myself dreading those days. Every so often when I stare into her black-brown eyes, I swear I can see them trembling just a little, like her eyeballs are about to become unhinged in their sockets and start rolling around. That scares me, and I can't help but think about what Jake said. Does she have some kind of disease? A brain tumor? Whatever it is, Hannah doesn't say, and I don't ask. It doesn't matter anyway. We are inseparable.

We have a routine. Every morning she bounces into my room and wakes me and Mouse up, and we all go to breakfast together and then to our classes. We always sit beside each other. Hannah doodles on my books, and we giggle until our teachers can't stand it anymore and we get separated. Then we write notes to each other and charm Mouse into passing them back and forth.

Hannah is so intense. When we find a minute to make out, I feel like the whole world disappears. She doesn't play games, like telling me she likes me and then acting aloof. No, there is none of that. She's an open book. She told me she loved me right away, and her notes are always romantic. An example:

Dear J,
I love your eyes. I love your lips.
I love your mind.
I want to be with you forever.
—H

I find myself looking forward to every new day at No Hope. I no longer wish to break free. I stop having trouble in class, and my therapy sessions with Jake are getting more productive.

Everything is going so great that when it suddenly stops, it comes as a real surprise. One morning I wake up and my redheaded alarm bell isn't in my room shaking me awake. It's quiet. I look over and see that Mouse is still asleep.

I dress and go across the hall to find Hannah. But she's not in her room, and her roommate—an ultra-religious girl named Susie—says she went to see the nurse.

I run down the hall to the medical office where we get our medicines and ice packs and band-aids and lice treatments. I see Jake coming out of the exam room. I run over to him. He puts his hands up.

"Jane," he says in his soothing voice. "Wait."

"Is Hannah in there?" I ask, peeking around him. Through the crack in the door I catch sight of her red hair, and she turns to look at me. Her face is blank, as if she doesn't recognize me, and her eyes are dead.

"Jane," says Jake. "Let's go."

"I-I don't understand," I say. "What's wrong? What happened to her?"

"It's okay," he says. "People with Hannah's condition sometimes have days like this. She will be fine soon, you'll see."

He leads me down the hall to the cafeteria and pushes me through the doors. "Jane," he says. "No matter what, you have to keep moving forward. I know you love Hannah, but you need to take care of yourself first. Got it?"

I nod. I hear his words, but my heart doesn't understand them. All I care about is her.

The next couple of days are agony, with Hannah holed up in her room. Then, suddenly, one morning she bursts into my room like nothing happened.

"Hey!" she says. "You miss me?"

"Y-yeah," I say, wiping the sleep from my eyes. "What happened, H?"

"Oh, nothing," she says quickly. "I just got a little sad because…"

"Because?"

"Jane," she says, and I can tell she has bad news. "I'm going home."

"What? When?" No, this cannot be happening.

"My parents are getting a divorce, and my mom wants me to come home. It was my dad who wanted me in here in the first place. He's moving in with some girlfriend of his, so I guess he doesn't care about me anymore."

"Whoa. I'm sorry. That's…that's—"

"Awesome!" she says.

I look at her, stunned.

"Yeah," she says. "Once I realized that I can stop playing by the rules and just be out—really out—in the world, it was like this huge weight lifted off me. I'll live with my mom, and I can be free to date whomever I want. And I want you, Jane."

She leans in to kiss me, and I am overcome with joy and sadness all at once.

"Wait," I say. "You're getting out. You're leaving me?"

She nods. "It's just for a little while. I'm going home, and then when you get out, you come and find me, and we will be together. Okay?"

"Okay," I say, then hesitate for a moment.

"What is it, babe?" She grins at me. "You worried about me?"

"No," I lie. "Okay, yes. It's just... you seemed so weird. Like you didn't even recognize me."

"I'm fine now," she says. "Finding out about my parents kind of wrecked me for a minute, but it's all good. Now," she says with a wicked smile, "how about we make the most of my time left, and I show you just how okay I am?"

We don't waste any time. My restrictions are lifted (thanks, Jake), and we go everywhere together—class, lunch, dinner, youth group, Bible study, church service. We don't care where we are as long as we're together. We sit together in the pews and use the hymnals to communicate secret messages by circling the letters in the songs. One day some No Hoper is going to open a hymnal and find some steamy lesbian love messages.

I'm allowed in Hannah's room as long as the door is open, and we borrow the school's portable stereo to play CDs from Hannah's collection. There are no MP3 players or phones allowed here, but Hannah gets a pass for music because it's considered part of her therapy. Most of her collection got confiscated during intake. No rock music (because

the devil) and no lesbian music (what-
ever that is) allowed. They let her keep
Chopin and some Leonard Cohen. I
guess she showed the intake team the
"Hallelujah" track and convinced them
Cohen was a safe bet.

Hannah loves her Leonard Cohen.
Her favorite lyric is the one where he
sings about a crack being in everything
and how, without that crack, the light
can't get in. Hannah says she's "super-
cracked" so she has more light inside
than most people. I believe her. I can
see it.

I decide that from now on I'm just
going to pray to Leonard Cohen. He's
the closest thing to God we have in here.

*Dear Leonard, please help me. These
people don't understand your poetry.
How will I survive? Also, what's the best
way to seduce Hannah?*

When we're not listening to Our
Lord Cohen on repeat, we make plans.

We talk about getting an apartment together. We draw pictures of what our home will look like. We imagine a shabby little place above a coffee shop where we'll work as baristas during the day. We'll write novels at night, and we'll look however we want and dress however we want and kiss each other out in the open. This promise to each other makes it a little easier to imagine getting through this place on my own.

The day Hannah is set to leave, the weather is humid. We go outside into the courtyard to stare at the mean gray sky.

"A storm is coming," says Hannah, her hair whipping around as the wind picks up. "We should go in." She turns to go, but I can't follow her.

"I'm afraid I'll never see you again." My voice comes out small and weird.

She turns to look at me. "Hey, it's okay," she says.

"Just stay with me," I plead.

"I can't."

"No, I mean stay with me here, outside, just for a while."

She looks at the sky. "It's going to rain." She smiles and shrugs.

We sit on the hard asphalt, cross-legged and back to back, our heads leaning toward each other as we look up. The clouds are moving faster now and the air is charged with a tinny taste and an electric feel. We watch as the storm rolls toward us, the steel-colored rain clouds booming with thunder. We just sit and let it come. At first there are a few small drops of rain and then we see a curtain wash toward us over the asphalt. Rain soaks our hair and clothes and we wait until the clouds pass overhead. We sit shivering for a long time, and then we get up to go. I look back over my shoulder as we approach the doors, the dry impressions we left on the pavement quickly disappearing as the rain takes them over.

I go to my room alone and change into dry clothes. I can't warm up. Hannah knocks on my door and then pokes her head inside. I sit on the bed and pat the mattress. She comes in and sits down, resting her head on my shoulder.

"I'm not going to do a whole big thing," she says. "I'm just going to leave. Because I can't handle that right now."

"Okay."

"You have to promise me something, Jane."

"Anything."

"No matter what happens when I'm gone, you have to keep going. You have to love yourself, Jane, because you are amazing. You're everything. You have to believe in yourself, Jane, the way I believe in you. You're going to be something special one day."

"Okay," I say, because it's all I can manage through the tears that are falling down my face. When Hannah says something, I believe it, because she always tells the truth.

When she leaves a few minutes later with promises to write, it's all I can do not to break down completely. For a little while I fantasize about escaping and running after her, but I know that's not what she'd want. I have to focus on the plans we made.

I have so much to look forward to. I can hardly wait.

Chapter Thirteen

The next several weeks are tough, but I put my head down and study, and I manage to pull up my grades to the point that Jake even asks me if I've thought about applying to college.

"College?" I ask. "Are you nuts?"

"No," he says. "I think you can do it. So let's say you decide to go for it. What would you study?"

"Well," I say, pretending I haven't thought about this before, "I kind of want to be a writer."

Jake smiles. "I think that's perfect for you. There's actually a decent program at Beacon. You could go part time to start. I've spoken to your parents, and I know they're on board with helping you with your tuition."

"Seriously?" I can't believe it.

"You've come a long way, Jane. Your dad and I have been speaking regularly, and he's very happy with your progress."

I nod. "I guess. The thing is, my plan is to get out and find Hannah. Then we're going to travel the world and maybe get married and maybe start a family. Or maybe none of that, I don't know. Maybe she'll come to college with me. Whatever it is, though, it will be with Hannah."

Jake smiles. "One thing at a time, okay? Why don't we fill out some applications? Cover your bases."

And just like that, my once dark and hopeless future has some bright new options. It's positively blinding.

Dad and Sheila come for a final visit, and it's as awkward as hell. Dad actually seems pretty relaxed and proud of me—he keeps reaching over and squeezing my shoulder. Sheila sits as far away from me as possible. She looks even skinnier than usual, like the corpse of an unhappy woman reanimated in Jake's office.

Jake's updating them on everything I've accomplished, and I notice that he keeps giving Sheila the side-eye.

"Wow, Janey, I'm so proud of you," my dad says when he hears about my improved grades.

"Thanks, Dad." I look at Sheila, but she says nothing. She just purses her lips even tighter, until her whole face seems pinched in.

Jake notices and clears his throat. "So, Sheila…" he begins.

"Mrs. Learning," she corrects him.

"Of course," says Jake.

Dad looks at Sheila, and I can see him bristle.

"Mrs. Learning," Jake starts again, "Jane is planning on studying creative writing at Beacon College this fall. Will she have a safe place to stay while she does that?"

"Safe?" asks Sheila. "What the fudge does that mean?"

"It means," says Jake calmly, "an environment free of judgment where she can focus on healthy behaviors. Can you provide that?"

"Janey is always welcome in our home," says Dad. I want to hug him.

Sheila shifts in her seat.

"Mrs. Learning?" asks Jake again.

"Sheila?" my dad prompts. "Answer him."

Sheila looks at Dad. "Listen, I know she's your daughter, but she's got so many problems. And she's...she's gay. I can't have that in my house. It's disgusting!"

The silence in the room is heavy. I find myself wishing Hannah was here. Hannah would know what to say.

"Dad?" I say. "It's okay. I understand. I can figure something else out."

Dad looks at me, then shouts, "Like hell!" Everyone jumps.

"John!" Sheila gasps.

"My daughter grew up in that house. That is *her* house. *Her* home. She belongs there with me. Hell, she's belonged there all this time, but I've been trying so hard to make you happy, Sheila. And you know what? Nothing will ever make you happy! You're just miserable."

Sheila is stunned. I am stunned. Jake just sits there with a little smile on his face.

"J-John," Sheila stammers.

"No, Sheila," he says. "Jane has been through so much, and I can't help but wonder if most of it is our fault."

My dad is crying now, something I have never seen, and it cuts me to the core.

"I'm sorry, Dad," I say. "This is my fault."

"No!" Dad grabs my hands in his. "This is on me. I'm so sorry I didn't support you. I don't want to hear you apologize for being who you are ever again. Do you hear me?"

I nod, because I can't speak.

But my dad is not done speaking. He turns to Sheila. "You have a choice, Sheila, one that you never gave to Jane. You can accept her and stay, or you can get the hell out."

I hide my crossed fingers behind my back.

Chapter Fourteen

Here's something awesome—no more Sheila. Here's something not so awesome—Dad got kicked out of our house and had to rent a crappy apartment. I don't really care, and I don't think he does either. He's been calling it "a fresh start" every time he calls me.

He checks in with me nearly every day now, and, with Jake's help, we're talking about our issues. I'm starting to understand how scared and lonely Dad was, and he's starting to understand how scared and lonely I was. Dad even says he'll drive me out to see Hannah once I get out, but only on the condition that in the meantime I study hard. I tell him I think I can do that for a couple more weeks. I haven't heard much from Hannah lately, and that kind of worries me. Her letters are coming less often now, and a couple of them were straight-up weird. I worry she's having a hard time on the outside. Jake tells me to be patient, to wait and see. Yeah, I'm not so good at that.

I don't have a lot of time to obsess about it, though, because I am busy getting my portfolio ready. I decide to take some of my journal entries and turn them into a longer story. It's a memoir, I guess, of my time at No Hope. I've been thinking, too, that even though this place is crazy, and I still don't buy into all the Bible stuff, maybe some of it isn't so bad. I might even have to rethink my nickname for it.

Finally, graduation day comes. There's no big ceremony. At No Hope, each kid graduates on their eighteenth birthday, all alone. I didn't get a cap and gown, but I do wear my best jeans. As I make my way down to the same administration office that processed my intake, I pull nervously at my shirt sleeves. Part of me is scared they will change their minds and have me committed for all eternity.

When I get to the office, I am relieved to see that Dad is already there waiting, and Jake is standing with him. I look past them into the open office door and see Pastor Jim inside, shuffling papers. I'm looking for red hair, listening for the sound of a cinematic voice, trying to feel if the energy in this space is charged. But there's none of that. Of course Hannah isn't here. Still, I hoped.

I look at Jake, and he shakes his head. "I haven't heard from her, Jane," he says, reading my mind in his freaky way.

"Ready to graduate, Graduate?" Dad jokes, but I can tell he's proud.

"Yeah, let's do this," I say, and I follow them into the office.

I get my diploma from Pastor Jim, and everyone shakes my hand like I'm an adult. It's bizarre. The whole time, I'm thinking about Hannah.

"Anything to say, Jane?" asks Jake.

"I don't know," I say, looking at them looking at me. "You'd think I did something amazing."

"You did," says Dad.

"Indeed," says Jake.

"Praise Jesus," says Pastor Jim, and Dad gives him a look.

I laugh in spite of myself.

"We're all very proud of you, Jane," says Jake.

"Thanks," I say, looking at my feet. Having people proud of me will take some getting used to.

"Now get out of here and don't ever come back," says Jake. He cracks a smile, and we all laugh, but I know what he means.

I take my diploma and follow Dad out through the unremarkable doors and to our car. I turn back and look at the building and marvel at how huge it seemed when I first came here. Now it looks so small. Jake is standing in the doorway, and he, too, looks even tinier than usual. He lifts his hand to wave. I wave back.

"Come on," says Dad.

I hop in.

"Let's put this place in our rearview mirror," he says and peels out of the parking lot.

And just like that we're off. Off to our new apartment. Off to my new life as a Baptist reform-school graduate. Off to Hannah, hopefully. Off to a future I can't even begin to imagine.

Chapter Fifteen

Dad was right about our new apartment. It totally sucks. It's tiny, there's no laundry, and the stove only has one working temperature: nuclear. No big deal though. We'll just be cramped and smelly, and all our dinners will be burned. At least we'll be together and happy.

For his part, Dad makes good on his promise and offers, the day after my graduation, to drive me out to see Hannah. I call ahead to make sure she's home, but no one answers.

"Let's go anyway," says Dad. "It'll be more romantic to just show up."

"Dad!"

"What? You want to do this or not?"

"I do."

"Then let's go. I'm dying to meet this redheaded goddess."

"Dad! I told you that if I let you read my portfolio, you could not use it against me."

Dad laughs. "Sorry, I couldn't resist. It's cute. Besides," he says, "your writing is really good, Jane. I can't wait until you get your acceptance letter."

Instantly my stomach is in knots.

Dad must notice my worried expression, because he is quick to reassure me.

"Hey," he says. "What does Jake say?"

I take a breath. "I know, I know. Stay in the moment. Try not to catastrophize."

"Okay," says Dad. "Now let's go get your girl."

We hurry out the door and hit the road.

It's a bit of a drive out to Hannah's place. She lives in a wealthy community about an hour or so from our crappy apartment.

When we finally arrive, I double-check the address against the envelope of one of her letters. The streets are dotted with stately homes boasting three-car garages and acres of perfect lawns.

"That's it," I say, pointing to a huge brown-brick home on the corner.

"Whoa," says Dad as he pulls up the car. "It's my dream house."

"Really? It's a bit big for my taste," I say. I know he's feeling down about the apartment.

"I didn't even know how to dream about a house like this," he says.

"Huh?"

"It's funny," Dad says. "You grow up a certain way, and you don't even know enough about yourself or the world to know what to dream for yourself. Or how to expect people to treat you."

"Dad? You okay?" I ask.

"Yeah, honey. I'm just figuring things out too, you know?" He turns the car off and looks at me. "I'll be here if you need me," he says, but I'm already hopping out of the car and hurrying up the long driveway.

I am so nervous. I haven't seen Hannah in a couple of months, and even though she said she loves me, her letters stopped coming. I can't help but worry she might have met someone else.

I take a deep breath and step up to the door. I ring the bell and wait.

After an eternity, a tall red-haired woman answers the door. She is obviously Hannah's mom.

I clear my throat. "Hi. You must be Mrs. Henriks," I say. "I'm—"

"Jane," she finishes, and her face goes white.

"Y-yeah," I say. "Is Hannah here?"

Mrs. Henriks closes her eyes for a long moment, and when she opens them I see that her eyes are rimmed with tears. I notice now for the first time that she is dressed in black, that her hair looks uncombed, and that there are several large flower arrangements on the front step.

"Jane," she begins, "I don't know how to tell you this. I'm sorry to tell you..."

"*Sorry*? What do you mean? Is Hannah okay?"

Mrs. Henriks shakes her head. "She's gone. My Hannah is gone."

"Gone? What do you mean, *gone*?"

I look past her into the house, but all I can see is a huge open staircase lined with immaculate white carpet. Hannah told me about this staircase. She said her room was at the very top of it. I have to find her.

With my heart in my throat, I lunge through the doorway. Mrs. Henriks gasps. I run toward the stairs.

"Jane, wait!" Mrs. Henriks calls from behind me, her voice strangled.

No, I can't wait. I have to find Hannah. I race up the stairs to the white door at the top of the landing. It's ajar. I push it open and step inside. I'm in Hannah's room, a place I've daydreamed about based on her descriptions. There's her four-poster bed, her writing desk, her wardrobe. But I don't see any of her posters, her books, her clothes. I don't see her. The room is filled with boxes. On the bedspread is a printed program. It has a photo of Hannah on it. I pick it up and then immediately drop it. It's a funeral program.

"No, no, no…" I hear my voice but can't feel it coming out of me. My chest tightens, and I can't breathe.

Dad comes up behind me. He stands close and places a hand on my shoulder. I jump from the shock of it.

"Jane, honey. Come now, baby. We should leave. Come home with me now." He leads me by the hand back down the long white staircase. Mrs. Henriks weeps silently as we pass.

"I'm so sorry," Dad whispers as we step through the doorway.

"Dad?" I ask, dazed. "Dad, what is happening?"

"Jane," he says, "try to breathe."

"We were going to get an apartment. We were going to buy all our stuff from thrift stores and eat noodles every night."

"I'm sorry, honey. I'm so sorry."

I collapse in his arms, and he carries me to the car.

For the first time since I was a little girl, I let go and cry hard. Not just a few tears, but huge, racking sobs. How can there be a world without Hannah?

When we get home, Dad calls Jake to see if he can get some answers. He talks for a long time in hushed tones. Eventually Dad sits down on the couch next to me and hands me the phone. I am so shredded, I don't know if I have the energy to speak.

"Jane," Jake says through the receiver. "I'm so sorry. We only just found out ourselves. Hannah's mother wanted to keep this private. I was going to call you today to see if we could meet. I didn't want to tell you over the phone."

"What happened?" I ask. "Did she—"

"She died by suicide, Jane."

I let the words sink in.

"Why?" I whisper, even though I know Jake won't be able to give me an answer.

"She was very ill, Jane. And she was in a lot of pain. Hannah had bipolar disorder, a very severe form, and when she was in a depression, it was very dangerous for her. There wasn't anything you could have done."

"But...but she said she loved me." I am crying again, the pain ripping through me.

"I know," says Jake. "And she did. She did love you. But she was hurting, Jane, and this had nothing to do with you."

Jake asks to speak to Dad again, and when Dad hangs up he looks really worried.

"What did he say?" I ask.

Dad hesitates. "He said to watch you closely...so that you don't..."

"You're afraid I'll do it too," I say, the realization dawning on me.

Dad just stares at me, like he's afraid to say it out loud.

"Dad," I say. "No matter what, I will never do that to you. Okay? You need to believe me. I know I scared you before. And I was careless, confused. But I couldn't do that. Not to you, not to me. I want...I want to live. Oh, Dad, why is this happening?"

Dad puts his arms around me. "I don't know. I wish I did. All I know is that I'm scared, Janey. I almost lost you once. I won't again. I'm going to stay with you right now. Every minute. Until we both feel a little less scared."

"Okay," I say.

Dad pulls a blanket up over both of us, and we spend the rest of the night on the couch, watching mindless TV. Eventually, with no tears left, I fall into a dark, dreamless sleep.

Chapter Sixteen

One day while I'm at the laundromat, washing our stinky clothes, two envelopes pop through the mail slot at our apartment. Dad collects them both and places them on the counter for me. They're the first thing I see when I walk through the door. Them and Dad pacing back and forth.

"Hey," he says.

"Hi. What are those, Dad?"

"Uh, you got mail. One letter is from Beacon College, and the other is from… from Hannah."

"What?" I race forward and scoop them up.

I scan the envelope with Hannah's return address and see that the letter has been redirected several times.

"I guess because we moved," Dad says by way of explanation, but I am way ahead of him.

I race to the bathroom and lock the door.

I tear open the envelopes. The letter from Hannah doesn't say much. It's a series of weird doodles and the words *love* and *sorry* all over the place, but there's no goodbye and no explanation. If anything, it's evidence that she was really lost. I brush a tear away and smell the paper, hoping for a hint of her green-apple perfume. It just smells like paper.

Dad knocks on the door. "You okay?"

"Yeah," I manage. "I'm okay."

I can hear him shuffling outside, and I decide to put him out of his misery. "I'm opening the letter from Beacon now, Dad."

I open the precisely folded official stationery and see the words:

> *Dear Miss Jane Learning,*
> *We are pleased to inform you...*

I scream and run out of the bathroom, nearly knocking Dad over in the process.

"I got in," I say. "I'm going to college!"

Dad grabs me in a bear hug, and we dance around for a while.

Once we calm down, he looks at me and asks, "Hannah?"

I shake my head. "No answers there, Dad. There never will be. I think from now on I'm just going to try to remember the good things."

"That sounds like a smart idea," he says.

"I know another smart idea," I offer.

"What's that?"

"Take me out for dinner to celebrate? I'm thinking pizza and ice cream."

"You're on, college girl."

We laugh as we make our way out the door, but it's bittersweet. I have a feeling that a lot of things in my life are going to be like that, and not just because of Hannah.

I'll go to college, and maybe I'll be a writer. Maybe I'll fall in love with another girl the way I did with Hannah, and maybe I won't. There will be good things. And there will be hard times too. I'm starting to understand that that's okay.

Chapter Seventeen

Sometimes when I'm sitting in my creative writing classes and I feel a bit lonely, I imagine Hannah sitting with me and making me laugh. I like reading the stuff the other students write, and every day that goes by brings me closer and closer to a real future as a writer. It makes me sad, too, to think that Hannah won't get to live in that future.

Then I remember her telling me everything will be okay. Sometimes I believe it, but faith is slippery. It's like sand falling through my fingers. Or those bubbles that floated over the world. I have to remind myself of the truth every day. When I need to know what's real, I just open my journal and visit with the Hannah I hold in my heart. I concentrate on the details of her face, her dark eyes, her wild red hair, the energy that lived in her. Every night I sit down to read the story of how one red-haired girl changed my life—a life I wasn't really living until she walked in.

I take a breath and close my eyes. I know I will be okay. And you will too.

ACKNOWLEDGMENTS

It is important to note that I am able to write books because I benefit from the love and support of my husband, Robert, and our children. Everything flows from that.

Thank you to Andrew Wooldridge for giving this story a shot, and to Tanya Trafford, my editor (and "dream-fulfiller"), for making it better.

I'd like to express my gratitude to the team at Orca Book Publishers for their hard work and dedication to publishing diverse books for teens.

This story is for my friends, the misfits, my kindred spirits and my chosen family. You keep me going.

Brooke Carter is a Canadian novelist and poet. She was born and raised in beautiful British Columbia, where she earned an MFA in Creative Writing (UBC). She is also the author of the Orca Soundings title *Another Miserable Love Song* and the forthcoming *Lucky Break* from Orca Sports. For more information, visit www.BrookeCarter.com.